TALES
FROM THE
CR

D0591619

TALES FROM THE CRYPT

Graphic Novels Available
from Papercutz

Graphic Novel #1
"Ghouls Gone Wild!"

Graphic Novel #2
"Can You Fear Me Now?"

Graphic Novel #3
"Zombielicious"

Coming July 2008: Graphic Novel #4
"Crypt-keeping it Real"

TALES FROM THE CRYPT

NO. 3 – *Zombielicious!*

NEIL KLEID	CHRIS NOETH
MARC BILGREY	MR. EXES
ROB VOLLMAR	TIM SMITH 3
JARED GNIEWEK	JAMES ROMBERGER
JIM SALICRUP	RICK PARKER
Writers	Artists

MR. EXES
Cover Artist

Based on the classic EC Comics series.

PAPERCUTZ™
New York

"EXTRA LIFE"
NEIL KLEID — Writer
CHRIS NOETH — Artist
MARK LERER – Letterer

"THE QUEEN OF THE VAMPIRES"
MARC BILGREY — Writer
MR. EXES — Artist
MARK LERER — Letterer

"GRAVEYARD SHIFT AT THE TWILIGHT GARDENS"
ROB VOLLMAR — Writer
TIM SMITH 3 — Artist
MARK LERER — Letterer
DIGIKORE — Colorist

"KID TESTED, MOTHER APPROVED"
JARED GNIEWEK — Writer
JAMES ROMBERGER — Artist
MARK LERER — Letterer
MARGUERITE VAN COOK — Colorist

GHOULUNATIC SEQUENCES
JIM SALICRUP – Writer
RICK PARKER – Artist, Title Letterer, Colorist
MARK LERER – Letterer

PREVIEW OF "JUMPING THE SHARK"
ARIE KAPLAN – Writer
MR. EXES – Artist
MARK LERER — Letterer

JOHN McCARTHY
Production

JIM SALICRUP
Editor–in–Chief

ISBN 10: 1-59707-090-4 paperback edition
ISBN 13: 978-1-59707-090-4 paperback edition
ISBN 10: 1-59707-091-2 hardcover edition
ISBN 13: 978-1-59707-091-1 hardcover edition

10 9 8 7 6 5 4 3 2

THE CRYPT OF TERROR

WELCOME TO THE *CRYPT OF TERROR*, HORROR FIENDS! YES, IT'S *ME* AGAIN... *THE CRYPT-KEEPER!* BACK AGAIN TO HOST MY TERROR-TOME, *TALES FROM THE CRYPT!*

NOW, IT MAY LOOK LIKE I'VE HIT BOTTOM, LAYING HERE IN THIS *GRUESOME OPEN GRAVE*, BUT THE *TERRIFYING* TRUTH IS I'M REALLY BACK IN THE *CRYPT OF TERROR*. YOU'RE JUST LOOKING AT THE *VIRTUAL* CRYPT-KEEPER!

YOU SEE, I'VE JUST GOT TO GET AWAY FROM THE *OLD WITCH* AND THE *VAULT-KEEPER!* EVER SINCE THE *UNSPEAKABLE* HAPPENED BACK IN THE 50s, THOSE TWO HAVE BEEN BUZZING AROUND ME LIKE *FLIES* OVER A *FRESH CORPSE!* THEIR CONSTANT JIBBER-JABBER HAS DRIVEN ME BACK TO AN *EARLY GRAVE!*

BUT EVEN THOUGH YOUR OL' FIEND, THE CRYPT-KEEPER MAY ENGAGE IN SUCH *ESCAPISM* TO AVOID THOSE *GHOULUNATICS*, I STILL KNOW WHAT'S *REAL* AND WHAT'S *NOT*--SOMETHING OUR FRIEND *ANDY DABBSTEIN* STRUGGLES WITH IN A TALE I CALL...

EXTRA LIFE!

I'VE BEEN DEAD FOR HOURS.

KILLED BY MY FRIENDS, ROBBED OF EVERYTHING I OWNED, I'M THE LATE, ONCE-GREAT, ANDY DABBSTEIN.

AND SITTING HERE -- SCARED AND SWEATING-- ALL I CAN THINK ABOUT IS HOW TO STOP IT FROM HAPPENING AGAIN.

HOW TO STOP IT FROM HAPPENING FOR REAL.

I WAS BORN ANDREW FRANCIS DABBSTEIN BUT I HAD A SECOND NAME. A SECOND LIFE.

LIVING TWO LIVES WASN'T EASY. ALMOST LIKE A CHEATER, JUGGLING TO KEEP A WIFE AND GIRL-FRIEND APART.

I NEVER CHEATED ON *CAMMY*, THOUGH. SHE KNEW EVERY DETAIL ABOUT MY LIFE...AND MY OTHER LIFE.

EVEN THE WOMEN THERE.

CAMMY'S GONE NOW. AS ARE THE OTHER WOMEN. THEY'RE GONE AND I'M DEAD.

I WAS HONEST TO THEM ABOUT MY DUAL LIVES AND BECAUSE OF THAT, MY WORLDS COLLIDED.

BECAUSE OF THAT I WAS KILLED ON THE BALROGTH PLAINS.

ONLINE, I WAS *EVENBLADE*, A LEVEL TEN PALADIN.

EVENBLADE ROAMED THE OGRE CONTINENT, SEARCHING FOR ADVENTURE.

12   2111

OFFLINE, I WAS ANDY. WORKER ANDY. LOYAL BOYFRIEND ANDY. GOOD OL', NOBODY ANDY.

I HATED ANDY.

I SPENT MORE TIME IN MY EXTRA LIFE THAN WITH ANDY'S APARTMENT, ANNOYED GIRLFRIEND AND TEDIOUS JOB.

EVENBLADE HAD A LOYAL FELLOWSHIP OF FRIENDS. EVENBLADE HAD A CAVE OF RICHES. EVENBLADE HAD HIS ADMIRING GIRLFRIEND, *KYRA RAVENHAIR*.

I HAVE NONE OF THOSE THINGS NOW. ANDY'S *OR* EVENBLADE'S.

AND SOON... SOON, I WON'T EVEN HAVE ME.

22   84

CAMMY DIDN'T LIKE EVENBLADE. SHE WAS AN ANDY GIRL.

THAT SUNDAY, THOUGH, SHE *HATED* ANDY. HIS LACK OF DRIVE. HIS LACK OF INITIATIVE.

I NEVER UNDERSTOOD THAT. EVENBLADE HAD INITIATIVE AND SHE HATED EVENBLADE.

SHE COULD BE SO *FRUSTRATING!*

THAT NIGHT IT WASN'T EVENBLADE WHO KILLED FIFTY BALTHGORIAN OGRES AND WON 800 GOLD P.

IT WAS *ANDY*.

THAT DAY, FOR THE FIRST TIME, ANDY WALKED THE BLASTED LANDS...AND SINCE OUR FELLOWSHIP SHARED A BOND, I UNBURDENED MYSELF TO THEM.

AS OUR PARTY EXPLORED THE OGRE CONTINENT, I EXPLAINED THE CAMMY SITUATION.

AND EVENBLADE PAID THE PRICE.

HIS GUARD DOWN, SOMEONE LIFTED 600 GOLD P FROM HIS CHAINLINK BELT.

ANDY'S WALLET WENT MISSING THE FOLLOWING MORNING.

WITHOUT A METROCARD OR CAB FARE, I HAD TO WALK TO WORK.

CAMMY WOULDN'T LOAN ME THE CASH. SHE WAS STILL ANGRY.

SHE BLAMED ME FOR LOSING THE WALLET, CALLING ME CARELESS AND IRRESPONSIBLE.

LATER THAT NIGHT, AS CAMMY SLEPT, ANDY UNBURDENED HIS HEART TO KYRA RAVENHAIR,

I REVEALED PERSONAL SECRETS I HADN'T TOLD ANYONE. EVEN CAMMY.

22   4411

WE ENCOUNTERED A WRAITH PACK IN THE THIRD CAVERN.

HORKUN THE MINOTAUR AND KYRA RETREATED, BUT *STEELHEART 67* AND I FOUGHT ON, EARNING 400P EACH.

12   8411

WHILE WE WAITED FOR THE REMAINING WRAITHS TO TIRE AND WANDER OFF, WE PASSED THE TIME.

AND THEN STEELHEART STARTED JOKING ABOUT SECRETS FROM ANDY'S PERSONAL LIFE.

SECRETS I HAD TOLD KYRA IN CONFIDENCE THE NIGHT BEFORE.

KYRA SAID SHE ASSUMED THE SECRETS WERE FAIR PLAY, LIKE WHEN I TOLD THEM ABOUT CAMMY...BUT I WAS *ANGRY!*

I WANTED TO KEEP ANDY'S AND EVENBLADE'S WORLDS AS SEPARATE AS POSSIBLE.

STEELHEART67 WAS SO ABSORBED IN OUR ARGUMENT...

...THAT HE NEVER NOTICED THE WRAITHS SNEAKING UP THE SIDE OF THE CAVERN.

HORKUN AND I FOUGHT THEM BACK, BUT IT WAS TOO LATE.

MY PROBLEMS HAD COST STEELHEART67 HIS ARM.

AND THE NEXT DAY, HE WAS GONE.

WOUNDED AND DISILLUSIONED, STEELBLADE67 RAN A SOLO CAMPAIGN AND WAS KILLED BY A HORDE OF GOBLINS.

KYRA AND I AVOIDED EACH OTHER. SHE WAS MORTIFIED AND I FELT BETRAYED.

12   8211

FEELING UNINSPIRED, I LEFT EARLY FOR WORK.

CAMMY'D BEEN GONE FOR HOURS AND SINCE WE COULDN'T SHARE A CAB, I TOOK THE 'A' TRAIN.

MY HEAD WAS SO FILLED WITH KYRA'S BETRAYAL THAT I DIDN'T NOTICE PEOPLE LAUGHING AT ME UNTIL THE TRAIN PULLED INTO THE STATION.

ONE OF THE MEN BEHIND ME WHISPERED SOMETHING TO HIS FRIEND, A LITTLE SECRET JOKE.

BUT IT WAS NO SECRET TO ME.

HE WAS WHISPERING A PRIVATE FANTASY I'D TOLD KYRA THE OTHER NIGHT. ONE OF THE SECRETS THAT HAD COST STEELBLADE67'S LIFE.

FUMING, I ASKED HIM HOW HE KNEW ?! WHO HAD TOLD HIM?

DID HE WALK THE OGRE CONTINENT? DID HE KNOW KYRA? WAS HE STEELBLADE67?

BUT HE JUST LAUGHED AT ME.

THE HARDER HE LAUGHED, THE ANGRIER I GOT.

ANDY WAS HURT AND BETRAYED.

EVENBLADE WAS HURT AND BETRAYED.

AND, LIKE STEELHEART67, SOMEONE ELSE PAID THE PRICE.

SOMEONE IN ANDY'S WORLD DIED AT EVENBLADE'S HANDS.

SOMEONE DIED BECAUSE I COULDN'T KEEP MY LIVES APART.

MY SECRETS HAD KILLED TWO PEOPLE, EACH IN A DIFFERENT WORLD.

EVENTS IN EVENBLADE'S LIFE WERE AFFECTING ANDY'S AND THE ANSWERS COULD ONLY BE FOUND ONLINE.

HORKUN CONFIRMED IT AFTER OUR DISASTROUS HUNT, SHE'D CANCELLED HER OGRE CONTINENT SERVICE. AS FAR AS WE MATTERED, KYRA RAVENHAIR NO LONGER EXISTED.

EVENBLADE'S GIRL-FRIEND NO LONGER EXISTED.

KYRA WASN'T IN THE PALADIN'S KEEP.

THE STAFF HADN'T SEEN HER FOR HOURS AND HER OGREMAIL ACCOUNT WASN'T WORKING.

...MY GIRLFRIEND NO LONGER EXISTED....

CAMMY.

CAMMY'S CELL PHONE DIDN'T WORK. NO SUCH NUMBER.

HER JOB HAD NO RECORD OF HER AND HER MOM DIDN'T KNOW WHO I WAS. SHE ASKED IF THIS WAS A JOKE...SHE HAD TWO SONS, NO DAUGHTERS.

ON MY WAY OUT, THREE PEOPLE CALLED ME BY A PRIVATE NICKNAME I'D ONLY REVEALED TO KYRA.

THE CRAZY OLD MAN WHO BEGS ON OUR STOOP ASKED AFTER HORKUN THE MINOTAUR.

DESPERATE, I WENT TO HER OFFICE BUT OF COURSE SHE WASN'T THERE.

I DEMANDED TO SEE HER DESK, SEE HER BOSS, SEE ANYTHING THAT WOULD PROVE ME WRONG.

I HAD TO KNOW.
I HAD TO KNOW.

HER DESK. I RAN PAST THE RECEPTIONIST, HOPING TO FIND CAMMY AT HER DESK.

INSTEAD, I FOUND TYLER.

TYLER WAS SITTING IN CAMMY'S DESK. HE SAID THAT HE'S BEEN OCCUPYING THIS DESK FOR TWO MONTHS.

TYLER STERNBERG
MARKETING

EXIT

AS SECURITY DRAGGED ME FROM THE BUILDING, TYLER GOT OFF THE TELEPHONE LONG ENOUGH TO SMILE, WINK, AND THROUGH THE ECHOING SILENCE IN MY EAR I HEARD HIM SAY:

"GOOD TO MEET YOU, BUDDY."

"MY BEST TO EVERYONE AT THE PALADIN'S KEEP."

CAMMY'S THINGS WERE GONE BY THE TIME I GOT HOME.

AT FIRST I THOUGHT SOMEONE MIGHT HAVE TAKEN THEM... BUT THERE WASN'T EVEN ANY DUST, ANY FILTH LEFT BEHIND. IT WAS AS IF CAMMY HAD NEVER LIVED HERE.

AS IF SHE HAD NEVER EXISTED.

AFTER THAT, I DIDN'T FEEL LIKE BEING ANDY VERY MUCH.

NO SECRETS. NO MONEY. NO GIRLFRIEND. IT WAS HARDLY LIVING.

TO BE HONEST, I DIDN'T FEEL LIKE SPENDING TIME IN EVENBLADE'S LIFE, EITHER.

THERE WAS SO MUCH OF ANDY IN IT THAT IT HARDLY FELT ADVENTUROUS AND INSPIRING.

MY JOB FIRED ME THE FOLLOWING MORNING.

I SEARCHED FOR A COROLLARY TO EVENBLADE'S LIFE BUT CAME UP EMPTY.

IN FACT, HORKUN SUGGESTED WE REFILL OUR FELLOWSHIP AND CHEER ME UP WITH AN ADVENTURE.

AFRAID OF THE CONSEQUENCES, I SAID NO... BUT TO BE HONEST, I WAS BORED WAITING FOR ANSWERS THAT WEREN'T COMING.

AND, OF COURSE, NEVER WOULD.

IT WAS EVENBLADE THE PALADIN, EVENBLADE THE STRONG, WHO WENT INTO BATTLE...

...BUT IT WAS ANDREW FRANCIS DABBSTEIN THAT DIED, STRUCK FROM BEHIND ON THE BALROGTH PLAINS.

THAT WAS TWELVE HOURS AGO.

I'D DIED ON THE OGRE CONTINENT. ONE OF MY LIVES HAD BEEN KILLED.

AND IT WAS A MATTER OF TIME BEFORE SOMETHING CAME FOR THIS ONE, TOO.

I WAS ALWAYS HONEST ABOUT MY WORLDS, MY TWO LIVES...AND BECAUSE OF THAT, THEY COLLIDED.

BECAUSE OF THAT, CAMMY WAS GONE. BECAUSE OF THAT I'M DEAD.

ANDY IS DEAD. AND NOW, I FINALLY UNDERSTAND WHAT IT IS TO LIVE.

I WAS BORN ANDREW FRANCIS DABBSTEIN BUT I HAD A SECOND NAME. AN EXTRA LIFE.

ALWYN IS A SMALL COLLEGE IN THE BERKSHIRE MOUNTAINS OF MASSACHUSETTS. IT'S QUIET, PICTURESQUE AND VERY OLD. MOST OF THE STUDENTS ON CAMPUS TALK ABOUT THE USUAL THINGS THAT YOUNG PEOPLE TALK ABOUT....

HEY, CHECK HER OUT.

SHE'S HOT!

THESE BOYS ARE LIKE SO IMMATURE!

WHICH BRINGS US TO THE DORM OF TWO ROOMMATES, SALLY "SYBIL" MILLS AND TINA "TANITH" BENSON, WHO ARE TALKING ABOUT THEIR FAVORITE SUBJECT...

GUESS WHAT I GOT, TANITH? VICTORIA PRICE'S NEW VAMPIRE DUBOIS NOVEL, "BOUQUET OF BLOOD"!

THAT'S NOT DUE OUT TILL NEXT MONTH! HOW'D YOU GET IT?

IT'S AN ARC--AN ADVANCE READING COPY! I POSED AS THE ALWYN CAMPUS NEWS' BOOK CRITIC.

YOU'RE BAD! C'MON LET'S READ IT!

VICTORIA PRICE
BOUQUET
BLOOD

WONDER WHY EVERYONE THINKS WE'RE WEIRD?

'CAUSE WE'RE IN A CEMETERY AT NIGHT, DRESSED LIKE VAMPIRES? SEEMS PERFECTLY NORMAL TO ME.

AS THE WEEK WORE ON...

LOOK AT HER, TELLING ANYONE WHO'LL LISTEN ABOUT WINNING THE CONTEST.

I SHOULD BE THE ONE WHO GETS TO MEET VICTORIA PRICE--NOT HER.

IF ONLY THERE WAS SOME WAY THAT I COULD GO THAT NIGHT INSTEAD OF TANITH.

CRACKKKK!

THE NEXT DAY, SYBIL, ARMED WITH TANITH'S I.D., BEGINS THE DRIVE TO BOSTON.

WISH ME LUCK, DEAR TANITH, WHEREVER YOU ARE. AS THE VAMPIRE DUBOIS SAID, IN *CONNOISSEUR OF BLOOD*, WHEN HE DROVE INTO BOSTON, TO MEET THE ILL-FATED ELIZABETH VANDERVEER, THE LOVE OF HIS LIFE...

"IN THE BEGINNING OF THE JOURNEY, I SAVOR THE ANTICIPATION AS IF IT IS A FINE WINE TO BE IMBIBED IN VERY SMALL SIPS."

HOURS LATER...

"BEHOLD," SAID THE VAMPIRE DUBOIS, "THE LIGHTS OF THE CITY BECKON ME LIKE THE SIRENS OF ULYSSES. BUT I FEAR THEM NOT, FOR I AM THE ONE WHO SHALL TRIUMPH."

YOU WERE CHOSEN AS THE CONTEST WINNER BECAUSE, AFTER A BACKGROUND CHECK, IT WAS DETERMINED YOU HAVE NO LIVING RELATIVES.

BUT, BUT... I'M NOT...

TO ANSWER YOUR QUESTION, WHAT INSPIRED MY CHARACTER DUBOIS...

...IS LIVING ON THE CEILING.

AND, YOU KNOW... GET PAID FOR IT.

TO ANOTHER MAN, PERHAPS ALSO FRESHLY RELEASED FROM THE STATE PSYCHIATRIC WARD, TWILIGHT GARDENS MIGHT HAVE LOOKED LIKE A PLACE TO BEGIN REBUILDING HIS FUTURE.

YOU EVER USE A MOP BEFORE, THOMAS?

DUH, LIKE A MILLION TIMES.

BUT FOR THOMAS DONALLEY, FORMER GROCERY SACKER, FORMER MOMMA'S BOY, FORMER *MADMAN*...

START HERE AND ROSE'LL BE ALONG SHORTLY TO DIRECT YOU.

NO RUSH.

THIS FLOOR WILL TAKE A WHILE TO CLEAN *PROPERLY*.

IT WAS JUST ANOTHER PLACE TO BE LAZY AND STUPID.

THOSE GUYS AT THE GROUP HOME ARE NUTS

THIS JOB IS *TOTALLY* EASY.

AFTER A COUPLE OF PAYCHECKS, MAYBE I CAN AFFORD JUST ONE--

KICK!

NO ONE GETS PAID AT TWILIGHT GARDENS FOR LEANING ON A MOP!

AAAAAGH!

ONE HOUR AND TWENTY-THREE NAUSEATING MINUTES LATER...

ONCE THE WATER RUNNING OFF IS COMPLETELY CLEAR, YOU KNOW YOU GOT 'EM PROPERLY HOSED DOWN!

A PINCH OF SANITIZING DUST AND YOU'RE READY FOR THE NEXT BATCH.

THE WHA-?

YOU GET STARTED ON THESE AND I'LL COME CHECK ON YOU AFTER LUNCH!

YOU WANT ME TO BRING YOU SOMETHING?

OH. I SEE YOU'VE ALREADY EATEN.

NOT EXACTLY. THERE WAS THIS MONEY ON THE FLOOR OF HIS ROOM, SEE AND I--

NEVER MIND ALL THAT! COME *ON!*

BOYS!

BUT WHEN THEY ARRIVE...

I DON'T UNDERSTAND...

THAT BED WAS EMPTY, I SWEAR IT!

AND THIS MONEY YOU SAW?

WELL, IT WAS KIND OF DARK. IT'S NOT LIKE I--

TUT, TUT, MY GOOD LAD.

DON'T YOU FRET ONE BIT ABOUT YOUR BLOOD.

NO...

HELP... ME...

IT DOESN'T SOUND LIKE YOU'LL BE *NEEDING* IT WHERE YOU'RE HEADED ANYWAY...

A COUPLE OF COMMERCIAL BREAKS LATER...

WHEN WE LAST LEFT YOU, RANDY HAD MADE IT UP TO THE FINAL LEVEL ON THE SHOW--THE SHARK-INFESTED TANK!

SNAP!

SPLOOSH!

DON'T MISS TALES FROM THE CRYPT NO. 4
"CRYPT-KEEPING IT REAL"

WATCH OUT FOR PAPERCUTZ™

If this is your very first Papercutz graphic novel, then allow me, Jim Salicrup, your humble and lovable Editor-in-Chief, to welcome you to the Papercutz Backpages where we check out what's happening in the ever-expanding Papercutz Universe! If you're a long-time Papercutz fan, then welcome back, friend!

Things really have been popping at Papercutz! In the last few editions of the Backpages we've announced new titles such as TALES FROM THE CRYPT, CLASSICS ILLUSTRATED, and CLASSICS ILLUSTRATED DELUXE. Well, guess what? The tradition continues, and we're announcing yet another addition to our line-up of blockbuster titles. So, what is our latest and greatest title? We'll give you just one hint -- the stars of the next Papercutz graphic novel series just happen to be the biggest, most exciting line of constructible action figures ever created! That's right -- BIONICLE is coming! Check out the power-packed preview pages ahead!

Before I run out of room, let me say that we're always interested in what you think! Are there characters, TV shows, movies, books, videogames, you-name-it, that you'd like to see Papercutz turn into graphic novels? Don't be shy, let's us know! You can contact me at salicrup@papercutz.com or Jim Salicrup, PAPERCUTZ, 40 Exchange Place, Ste. 1308, New York, NY 10005 and let us know how we're doing. After all, we want you to be as excited about Papercutz as we are!

Thanks,

Jim

EDITOR-IN-CHIEF

Caricature drawn by Steve Brodner at the MoCCA Art Fest.

TWO DOZEN TEEN DETECTIVE GRAPHIC NOVELS NOW IN PRINT!

You know, while it's exciting to be adding so many new titles, we don't want anyone to think we've forgotten any of our previous Papercutz publications! For example, can you believe there are now two dozen all-new, full-color graphic novels starring America's favorite teen sleuths?! Let's check out what's happening in the 12th volume of NANCY DREW…

Writers Stefan Petrucha and Sarah Kinney and artists Sho Murase and Carlos Jose Guzman present Nancy's latest case, "Dress Reversal." After showing up at River Height's social event of the year, in the identical dress as the party's hostess, Deirdre Shannon, things get worse for Nancy when she's suddenly kidnapped! That leaves Bess, George, and Ned to solve the mystery of the missing Girl Detective.

That's all in NANCY DREW #12 "Dress Reversal," on sale sale at bookstores everywhere and online booksellers.

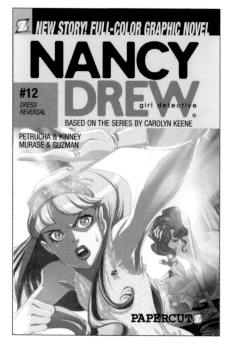

NEW STORY! FULL-COLOR GRAPHIC NOVEL

NANCY DREW girl detective®

#12
DRESS REVERSAL

BASED ON THE SERIES BY CAROLYN KEENE

PETRUCHA & KINNEY
MURASE & GUZMAN

PAPERCUTZ

Behold. . .

At the start of the new millennium, a new line of toys from LEGO made their dramatic debut. Originally released in six color-coded canisters, each containing a constructible, fully-poseable, articulated character, BIONICLE was an instant hit!

The BIONICLE figures were incredibly intriguing. With their exotic names hinting at a complex history, fans were curious to discover more about these captivating characters. Even now, over six years later, there are still many unanswered questions surrounding every facet of the ever-expanding BIONICLE universe.

A comicbook, written by leading BIONICLE expert and author of most of the BIONICLE novels Greg Farshtey, was created by DC Comics and given away to members of the BIONICLE fan club. The action-packed comics revealed much about these mysterious biomechanical (part biological, part mechanical) beings and the world they inhabited. A world filled with many races, most prominent being the Matoran. A world once protected millennia ago by a Great Spirit known as Mata Nui, who has fallen asleep. A world that has begun to decay as its inhabitants must defend themselves from the evil forces of Makuta.

The first story arc of the comics called "The BIONICLE Chronicles," begins when six heroic beings known as Toa arrive on a tropical-like island which is also named Mata Nui. The Toa may just be the saviors the people of Mata Nui need, if they can avoid fighting with themselves, not to mention the Bohrok and the Rahkshise early comics are incredibly hard-to-find, and many new BIONICLE fans have never seen these all-important early chapters in this epic science fantasy. But soon, those comics will be collected as the first two volumes in the Papercutz series of BIONICLE graphic novels.

These early comics are incredibly hard-to-find, and many new BIONICLE fans have never seen these all-important early chapters in this epic science fantasy. But soon, those comics will be collected as the first two volumes in the Papercutz series of BIONICLE graphic novels.

In the following pages, enjoy a special preview of BIONICLE graphic novel #1...

I HAVE SLEPT FOR SO LONG. MY *DREAMS* HAVE BEEN *DARK* ONES.

BUT NOW I AM *AWAKENED*.

NOW THE SCATTERED ELEMENTS OF MY BEING ARE REJOINED.

NOW I AM *WHOLE*.

AND THE *DARKNESS CANNOT STAND* BEFORE ME.

BIONICLE 1:

GREG FARSHTEY-WRITER
CARLOS D'ANDA-PENCILLER
RICHARD BENNETT-INKER
ALEX SINCLAIR-COLORIST

DON'T MISS BIONICLE GRAPHIC NOVEL # 1 "RISE OF THE TOA NUVA"

A SPECIAL EXCLUSIVE
NANCY
DREW
girl detective
BONUS FEATURE IN #12!

Writing Nancy Drew
becomes a family affair!

As all loyal Papercutz followers already know, Stefan Petrucha has been writing the NANCY DREW graphic novels since the very first volume. More recently, he's been joined by Sarah Kinney, and together they've been chronicling the latest mysteries of our favorite Girl Detective. Some fans have asked how the two talented writers actually are able to write together? Do they sit side-by-side at their computer keyboard typing together? Does Stefan write one word, then Sarah the next? Well, that actual process will remain a mystery for now, but what we will reveal is that these two are not only co-writers, but they're actually husband and wife.

But here's where the plot thickens (whatever *that* means!)... turns out one of their daughters recently completed a very interesting project in school. Everyone in Mrs. Schreiber's third grade class had to write and draw a Nancy Drew comic, and Margo Kinney-Petrucha's charming Nancy Drew adventure has just been published in the Backpages of NANCY DREW graphic novel #12 "Dress Reversal"! That's right, not only do you get a great story by Margo's mom and dad, but she also wrote, drew, lettered, and colored a six-page story that's really a lot of fun! Take a peek at the excerpt on the next page -- we think it's great! You may want to pick up a copy of NANCY DREW #12 just to have the comics debut of Margo Kinney-Petrucha. She may be the next award-winning graphic novelist someday.

ANNOUNCING THE WINNER OF THE "WRITE YOUR OWN NANCY DREW MYSTERY" CONTEST!

To celebrate last year's Nancy Drew movie, we held a super-special writing competition at papercutz.com. We asked all you clever Nancy Drew fans to start their stories with the first page from our biggest Nancy Drew graphic novel adventure, "The High Miles Mystery." But what if instead of going off on the mystery in graphic novels #9 - 11, Nancy, and her best friends Bess Marvin and George Fayne went on a completely different adventure to solve a mystery dreamed up by YOU?!

We got so many wonderful submissions, that it was really difficult to pick just one winner. Ultimately, we basically took all our favorites, put them all in a hat, and picked one at random. So, without further ado, we here at Papercutz are proud to announce that the winner is...

AMANDA GONZALEZ!!

Congratulations, Amanda!

One of the unique aspects of Amanda's entry was that she wrote it in script form, similar to how Nancy Drew's graphic novels and movies are written, and not like the Nancy Drew books available from Simon & Schuster and Grosset & Dunlap. And now, let's all enjoy Amanda's story...

The first page of "The High Miles Mystery," the basis for the contest.

Bess Marvin- Strange lights in these woods, are you sure about that, Nan?

Nancy Drew- I'm positive Bess, it says so in this paper. One individual clearly said that it's not any flashlights because these lights were far too powerful and appeared to look 'mystical' in some way, they were 'purple, green, and blue colored lights that glowed in a strange way' that's the exact quote from the paper. Here take a look...

George Fayne- Oh, come on, Nancy, do you really believe all that nonsense? It's probably just some local kid playing a prank and reporting these strange lights that they made up. Or maybe it's aliens coming to get us all right here in River Heights, and they're after Bess and all the snacks she carries around in her backpack.

Bess- Stop that, George! Nancy, you don't think it could really be aliens, do you?

George- I was kidding, Bess! It's not aliens, there is no such things as aliens or any of that nonsense stuff.

Nancy- All right, you guys, enough arguing. I've called you both here on this "camping" trip to help me investigate this mystery and get down to the real facts of this case.

(The three of them go into the woods in search of these strange mystical lights. While walking with their flashlights, George trips and falls.)

George- Ouch!

Nancy- George, are you okay?!

George- Yeah, I'm fine. Hey, you guys, look at this.

Bess- Hey, it's some kind of strange light bulb-- and look there is a line attached to it that leads deeper into the woods.

(The three of them follow the line to the center of the woods where they find a tree that was draped with lots of different types of lights.)

Nancy- Shhh....do you guys hear that? It sounds like footsteps. Come on over here, we can hide behind these trees.

(The three of them hide behind the trees and wait to see who appears. It is Mr. Daniels -- the local owner of the Camping Supplies store in town. The girls continue to watch as he sets up more lights and starts to play a tape that makes sounds like an animal growling and walking.)

Bess- What in the world is Mr. Daniels doing? Look, he's turning on a switch over there. Hey, look, the tree just lit up with all those strange light bulbs and they look exactly as the man in the paper said: "Mystical lights of blue, purple, and green colors."

George- Yeah, and listen, the tape sounds like some strange animal moving around, making noise.

(The girls step out and ask Mr. Daniels what he's doing. George has her cell phone and explains to him that she is going to call the police if Mr. Daniels doesn't tell them the truth and confess to the locals that he is the mastermind behind the mysterious lights in the woods that was terrifying the locals.)

Mr. Daniels- All right, girls, you caught me. I was the one who submitted that story to the papers secretly. I made up the story and created these strange colored lights, along with the tape because I wanted people to spread the story around to other neighboring towns so

as to gain publicity. I figured with all the attention, news stations would be coming up to check out the story.

Nancy- And in order to check the story out they would have to wait till dark to come into the woods. But they can't get into the woods and go camping unless they have the proper equipment to do so. This means they would need to go to your

Camping Supplies store in order to get those supplies.

Daniels- Yes, that's right. It's just that business has been so bad these days. Nobody seems to want to go camping and all the kids are interested in these days is the mall and going to that new theme park outside of town. I figured with all the attention, I could finally get some business and make a profit. I apologize and I promise I'll tell the local paper that the story was all false and tell everyone the truth.

(The girls help to clean up the campsite and they all head back into town. And, as promised, Mr. Daniels came clean and told everyone in River Heights the truth. He wrote to the paper and told the police as well that he was responsible for having created the story and having set up the lights in the woods.)

Bess- Yes!!! We did it, you guys! We solved the case of the mysterious lights in the woods.

George- Yup! Now River Heights knows the real story behind this case. And the kids don't have to be afraid to go camping. Actually, I saw that Mr. Daniels's store is doing quite well, and there are more kids then ever before going camping. So, I guess it all worked out in the end.

Nancy- Good job, you guys, thanks for the help. I couldn't have solved this case without you both.

Another case solved by super sleuth Nancy Drew and her friends Bess and George!

THE END!